A book based on a true story is best dedicated
to those whose reality provided the raw material.

For Ingeborg Schraft Hoffman, M.D.,
who waited many months for a new coat and who showed
it to me some twenty-five years later.

And in memory of her mother, Hanna Schraft,
who at the start of it all had nothing—save her
persistence and determination—and who in the end
fashioned a beautiful gift.

H.Z.

This is a Borzoi Book published by Alfred A. Knopf, Inc. Text copyright © 1986 by Harriet Ziefert. Illustrations copyright © 1986 by Anita Lobel. All rights reserved under International and Pan-American Copyright Conventions. Published in the United States by Alfred A. Knopf, Inc., New York, and simultaneously in Canada by Random House of Canada Limited, Toronto. Distributed by Random House, Inc., New York. Manufactured in the United States of America   10   9   8   7   6   5   4   3   2   1

Library of Congress Cataloging-in-Publication Data: Ziefert, Harriet. A new coat for Anna. Summary: Even though there is no money, Anna's mother finds a way to make Anna a badly needed winter coat. [1. Coats—Fiction] I. Lobel, Anita, ill. II. Title. PZ7.Z487Ne   1986   [E]   86-2722
ISBN 0-394-87426-9   ISBN 0-394-97426-3 (lib. bdg.)

A New Coat for Anna

by Harriet Ziefert · pictures by Anita Lobel

Alfred A. Knopf ✎ New York

Winter had come and Anna needed a new coat. The fuzzy blue coat that she had worn for so many winters was no longer fuzzy and it was very small.

Last winter Anna's mother had said, "When the war is over, we will be able to buy things again and I will get you a nice new coat."

But when the war ended the stores remained empty. There still were no coats. There was hardly any food. And no one had any money.

Anna's mother wondered how she could get Anna a new coat. Then she had an idea. "Anna, I have no money," she said, "but I still have Grandfather's gold watch and some other nice things. Maybe we can use them to get what we need for a new coat. First we need wool. Tomorrow we will visit a farmer and see about getting some."

The next day Anna and her mother walked to a nearby farm.

"Anna needs a new coat," Anna's mother told the farmer. "I have no money, but I will give you this fine gold watch if you will give me enough wool from your sheep to make a coat."

The farmer said, "What a good idea! But you will have to wait until spring when I shear my sheep's winter wool. Then I can trade you their wool for your gold watch."

Anna waited for spring to come. Almost every Sunday she and her mother visited the sheep. She would always ask them, "Is your wool growing?" The sheep would always answer, "Baaa!" Then she would feed them nice fresh hay and give them hugs.

At Christmastime Anna brought them paper necklaces and apples and sang carols.

When spring came the farmer sheared the sheep's wool.

"Does it hurt them?" asked Anna.

"No, Anna," said the farmer. "It is just like getting a haircut."

When he had enough wool to make a coat, the farmer showed Anna how to card the wool. "It's like untangling the knots in your hair," he told Anna.

Then he gave Anna's mother a big bag of wool and Anna's mother gave him the gold watch.

Anna and her mother took the bag of wool to an old woman who had a spinning wheel.

"Anna needs a new coat," Anna's mother told the woman. "I have no money, but I will give you this beautiful lamp if you will spin this wool into yarn."

The woman said, "A lamp. That's just what I need. But I cannot spin quickly, for I am old and my fingers are stiff. Come back when the cherries are ripe and I will have your yarn."

When summer came, Anna and her mother returned. Anna's mother gave the old woman the lamp and the old woman gave them the yarn— and a basket of delicious red cherries.

"Anna, what color coat would you like?" Anna's mother asked.

"A red one!" Anna answered.

"Then we will pick some lingonberries," said Anna's mother. "They make a beautiful red dye."

At the end of summer, Anna's mother knew just the place in the woods to find the ripest lingonberries.

Anna and her mother boiled water in a big pot and put the berries into it. The water turned a deep red. Anna's mother dipped the pale yarn into it.

Soon red yarn was hanging up to dry on a clothesline strung across the kitchen.

When it dried, Anna and her mother wound the yarn into balls.

They took the yarn to the weaver.

"Anna needs a new coat," Anna's mother said. "I have no money, but I will give you this garnet necklace if you will weave this yarn into cloth."

The weaver said, "What a pretty necklace. I will be happy to weave your yarn. Come back in two weeks."

When Anna and her mother returned, the weaver gave them a bolt of beautiful red cloth. Anna's mother gave the weaver the sparkling garnet necklace.

The next day Anna and her mother set off to see the tailor.

"Winter is coming and Anna needs a new coat," Anna's mother told the tailor. "I have no money, but I will give you this porcelain teapot if you will make a coat from this cloth."

The tailor said, "That's a pretty teapot. Anna, I'd be very happy to make you a new coat, but first I must take your measurements."

He measured her shoulders. He measured her arms. He measured from the back of her neck to the back of her knees. Then he said, "Come back next week and I will have your coat."

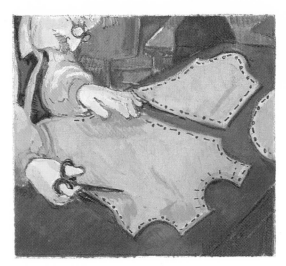 

The tailor set to work making a pattern, cutting the cloth, pinning, and sewing and stitching and snipping. He worked and worked for almost a whole week. When he was finished, he found six pretty matching buttons in his button box and sewed them on the coat.

He hung the coat proudly in the window for everyone to see.

When Anna and her mother returned to the tailor's shop, Anna tried on her new coat. She twirled around in front of the mirror. The coat was perfect!

Anna thanked the tailor. Anna's mother thanked him, too, and gave him the pretty porcelain teapot.

Anna wore her new coat home. She stopped at every store to look at her reflection in the window.

When they got home her mother said, "Christmas will soon be here, and I think this year we could have a little celebration."

Anna said, "Oh, yes, and please could we invite all the people who helped to make my coat?"

"Yes," said Anna's mother. "And I will make a Christmas cake just like I used to."

Anna gave her mother a big hug.

On Christmas Eve the farmer, the spinner, the weaver, and the tailor came to Anna's house. They all thought Anna looked beautiful in her new coat.

The Christmas cake that Anna's mother baked was delicious. Everyone agreed that this was the best Christmas they had had in a long time.

On Christmas Day Anna visited the sheep. "Thank you for the wool, sheep," she said. "Do you like my pretty new coat?"

The sheep seemed to smile as they answered, "Baaa! Baaa!"